Finley the Flute

by Claire Geddes

Illustrated by Noel Tuazon

MW00886297

Copyright © 2013 Claire Geddes

All rights reserved.

ISBN: 1482725606

ISBN-13: 9781482725605

Finley was a flute.

He was the only flute in a town of stringed instruments.

All around Finley were instruments that were made of wood and strings.

But Finley was different.
He was made of
silver and keys.

Finley was adopted.
His parents were violins.

His brother
Jimmy was a cello.

His parents and Jimmy played music together. It sounded so wonderful.

Dut Finley could only watch. He knew he was a
flute, and he knew flutes made music, but no one
showed him how to play music. They didn't know
how flutes worked.

What Finley wanted more than
anything was to play with
his family.

But his family only knew how
to play string music. And that
made Finley sad.

"Mom?" said Finley.

"Yes Finley?" his mom replied.

"Why am I *so* different from everyone?"

"Finley," his mother said, "You're not different. You are a special instrument.

"I know, I just wish I was like you, dad and Jimmy."

"One day you'll learn how to play your own beautiful music," Finley's mom said, stroking him with her bow, "and no orchestra will be complete without you."

Finley didn't believe his mom.

Upstairs, Jimmy was practicing his part for orchestra class. Finley pretended that he was a stringed instrument too and hummed along alone in his room.

At school, Finley was reminded that he didn't look like the stringed instruments. There were the hand-crafted violins, studious cellos, and imposing basses.

There was nothing in the world that Finley wanted more than to look and sound like everyone else. But he didn't have strings – he had keys and holes. What could he do with that?

During music class, the violins, violas, cellos and double basses played together. Finley hummed along, but was never more than an outsider.

The string orchestra was preparing for the big spring concert. It was the most important concert of the year.

Things were not going well in music class. Not everyone practiced their parts. The bass didn't sound quite right, and the violins could not reach the really high notes. They sounded like screechy cats. Finley sat in the corner, as he always did.

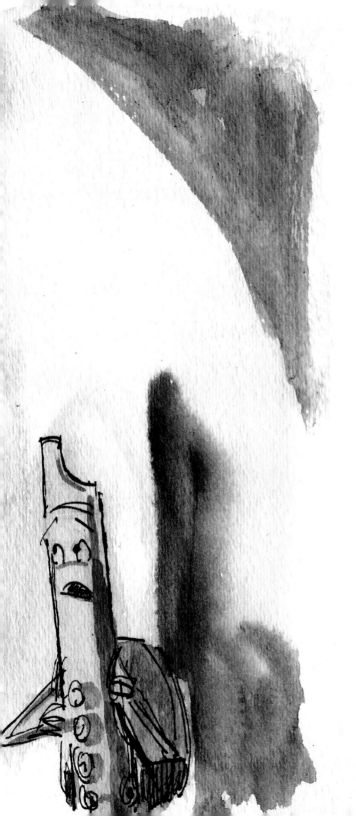

After school, Finley's brother Jimmy was talking to a violin.

"We have to hit those high notes, Jimmy. The concert will be ruined."

Finley was worried too. The violins never hit the high notes. It would make everybody look bad if they couldn't do it.

The next day in class, the violins missed their high notes. Finley hummed along. He hadn't noticed that the orchestra had stopped playing. He hit all the high notes.

"Finley, was that you?" the conductor asked.

"I'm sorry. I won't do it again." Finley said.

"No, do it again! Those were the notes we have been trying to hit!"

The conductor started the orchestra again. The violins played the melody, while the basses held up the low end. Finley knew the high notes were coming. His mouth got dry. Finley couldn't quite hit the notes.

"That's almost it, Finley. Try it again." the conductor said.

F inley tried again, but he still couldn't get the high notes. He felt like he let everyone down.

"Why don't you practice it at home Finley?" the conductor said.

"I will, I will!" Finley said.

"Play with us at the concert." the conductor said.

"Really?" asked Finley.

"Really, Finley. I heard you do it once. I know you can do it again." the conductor said.

At home, Finley practiced every moment he could. He practiced with Jimmy, instead of humming in the next room.

"Finley, that sounds wonderful." Finley's mom said.

"But I'm still not hitting the high notes." Finley said.

"But you are making your own music." Finley's mom said.

Soon, it was the night of the big concert. The whole school was there. Finley was so nervous. He knew the whole orchestra was depending on him. Finley looked over and saw Jimmy smiling at him.

Finley remembered that he hit the notes before. The time for Finley's part had come. He took a big breath and played all the notes perfectly. The audience was amazed.

Finley realized that being different made him special. After that, Finley played with his family every night.

THE END.

CPSIA information can be obtained
at www.ICGtesting.com
Printed in the USA
BVIC00n1706071213
338444BV00002B/46

9 781482 725605